Written and Illustrated by

RAYMOND BRIGGS

Jim and the Beanstalk

SCHOLASTIC INC.

New York   Toronto   London   Auckland   Sydney

ISBN 0-590-47723-4

Copyright © 1970 by Raymond Briggs. All rights reserved.
Published by Scholastic Inc., 730 Broadway, New York, NY 10003,
by arrangement with Sandcastle Books, a division of the
Putnam & Grosset Book Group.

12 11 10 9 8 7 6 5 4 3 2 1   3 4 5 6 7 8/9

Printed in the U.S.A.   08

First Scholastic printing, September 1993

Early one morning Jim woke up and saw a great plant
growing outside his window.
"That's funny," he said, "it wasn't there yesterday.

I'll see how high it goes," and he began to climb up the plant.

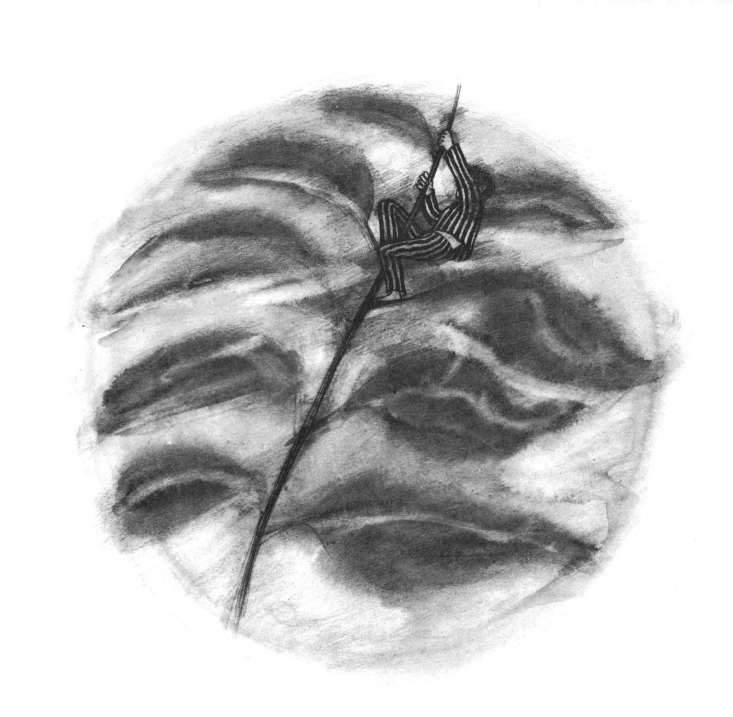

"It certainly is big," he said, as he disappeared into the clouds.

When he reached the top of the plant, Jim saw a castle. "I'm hungry," he said. "I'll ask at the castle for breakfast. I hope they have some cornflakes."

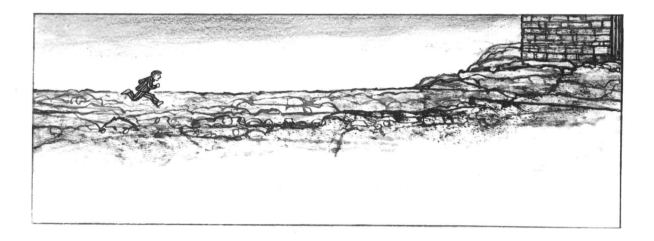

Jim ran to the castle and knocked on the door. He waited and waited, until the door was slowly opened by a very old giant.

"Aha!" said the Giant. "A boy. A nice juicy boy. Three fried boys on a slice of toast. That's what I used to enjoy eating in the old days, but I haven't any teeth now. Come in, boy. You're safe."

The Giant shared his breakfast of beef and beer with Jim.

"Is your name Jack?" he asked.

"No," said Jim, "it's Jim."

"Did you come up a beanstalk?" asked the Giant.

"I came up some sort of plant," said Jim.

"It's that beanstalk again," said the Giant. "It came up once before. That nasty boy Jack stole some of my father's gold and took our golden harp and our golden hen and I've never really been happy since. Now I'm old, too. I can't even see to read my poetry books because the print is too small."

"Don't you have any glasses?" asked Jim.

"Only beer glasses," said the Giant.

"I mean reading glasses," said Jim. "They go on your nose and ears."

"It's my eyes I'm talking about!" roared the Giant, banging his fist on the table.

"These glasses are *for* your eyes," said Jim, and he explained about glasses while the Giant listened carefully. "Get 'em!" said the Giant fiercely when Jim had finished. "Get 'em for me. I'll pay good gold."

"I'll have to measure you," said Jim.
So Jim measured the Giant's head.

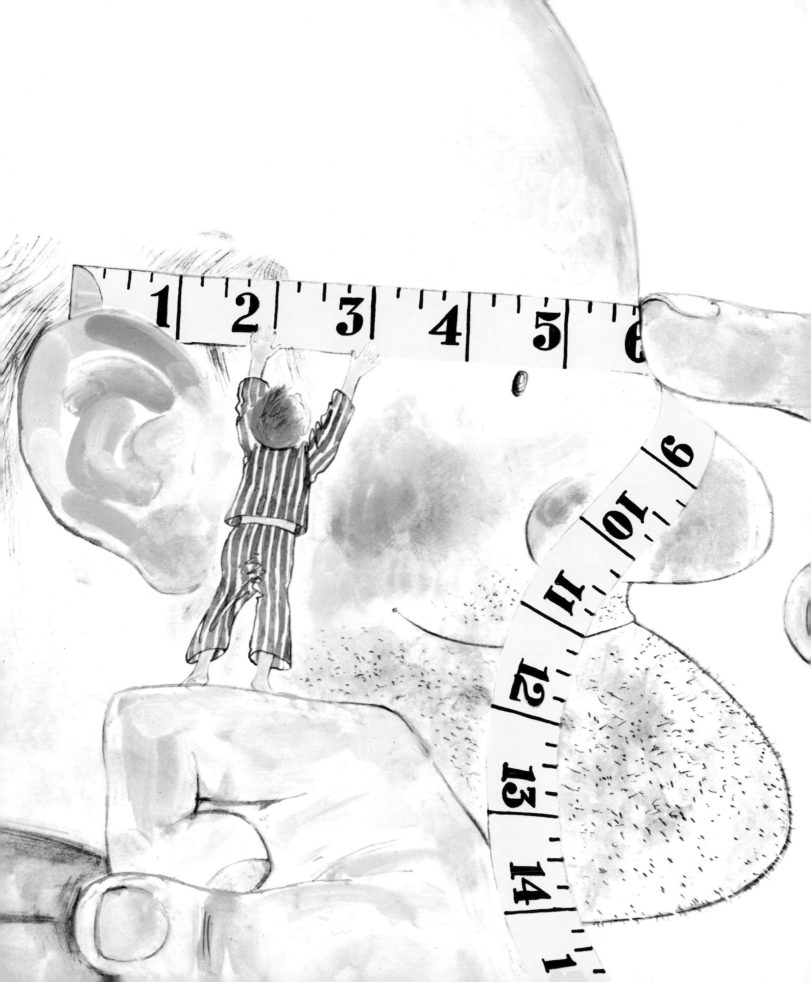

The Giant gave Jim a gold coin, and Jim climbed down the
beanstalk as fast as he could, holding tight to the coin.
He showed it to his mother, but before she could say
anything he got dressed and ran off to the oculist.

The oculist could hardly believe his eyes when he saw the giant gold coin, but he set to work straight away. He worked all night, and in the morning the glasses were ready.

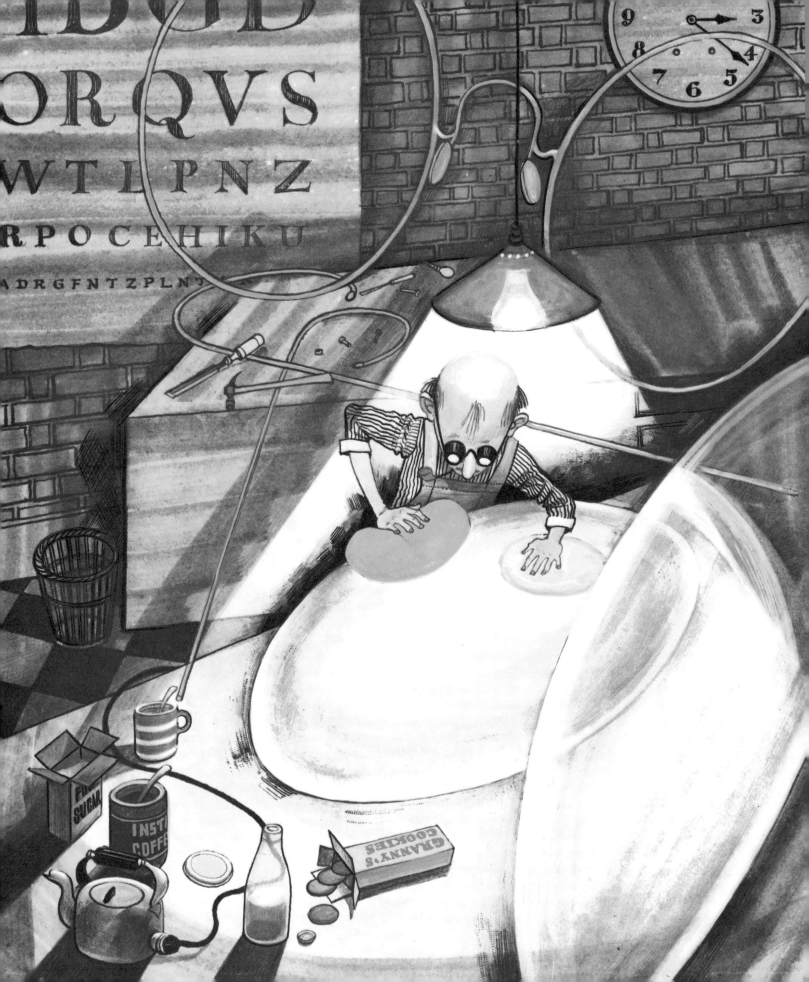

Jim carried them home. Then he tied them on his back and climbed up the beanstalk.

The Giant loved his glasses. He put them on and began reading rhymes to Jim.

"You're a good boy," he said. "Now I can see you properly. I wonder how juicy you are? I can't eat anything much nowadays because I don't have any teeth."

"Why don't you have false teeth?" asked Jim.

"False teeth!" roared the Giant. "Never heard of them!"

So Jim explained about false teeth while the Giant listened carefully.

"Get 'em!" said the Giant when Jim had finished. "Get 'em for me. I'll pay good gold."

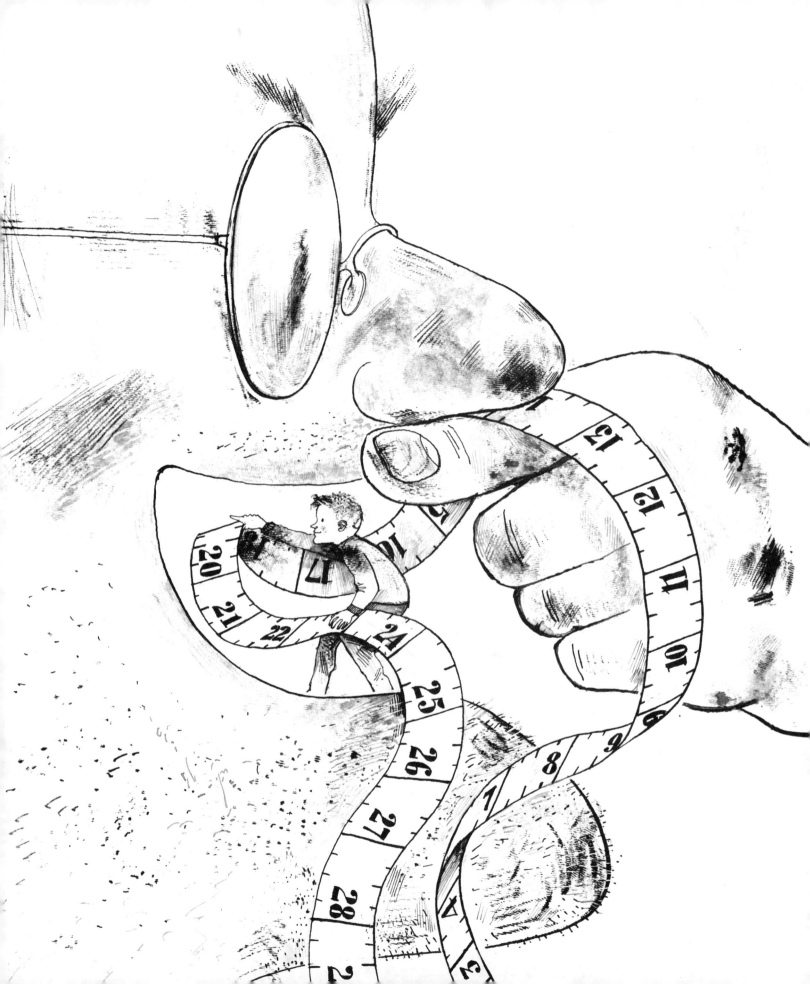

So Jim measured the Giant's mouth. "Make 'em big," said the Giant, "and sharp. I like sharp teeth."

The Giant gave Jim a gold coin and Jim climbed down the beanstalk as fast as he could, holding tight to the coin. He showed it to his mother, but before she could say anything he ran off to the dentist.

The dentist could hardly believe his eyes when he saw the giant gold coin, but he set to work straight away. He worked all night, and in the morning the teeth were ready. Jim carried them home. Then he tied them on his back and climbed up the beanstalk.

The Giant loved his new teeth. He jumped up and down,
chomping his jaws and gnashing the teeth until sparks
flew.

Then the Giant sat down, looked at himself in a mirror, and was suddenly sad again.

"Ah," he said, "I used to be a good-looking lad. Great head of flaming red hair I had, and now look at me."

"Why don't you have a wig?" asked Jim.

"A wig!" roared the Giant. "Never heard of a wig!"

So Jim explained about wigs while the Giant listened carefully.

"Get one!" said the Giant when Jim had finished. "Get one that's red and curly! I'll pay good gold."

So Jim measured the rest of the Giant's head.

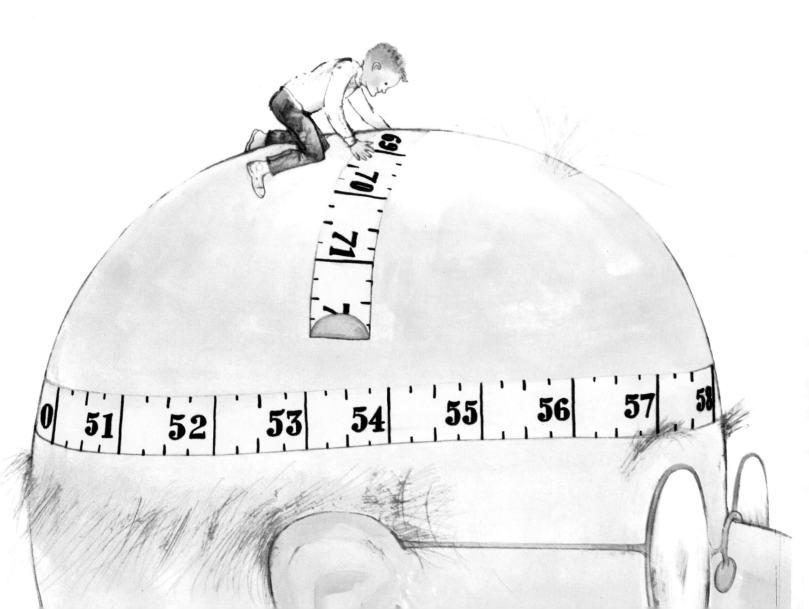

The Giant gave Jim a gold coin, and Jim climbed down the
beanstalk as fast as he could, holding tight to the coin. He
showed it to his mother, but before she could say anything
he ran off to the wig-maker.

  The wig-maker could hardly believe his eyes when he
saw the giant gold coin, but he set to work straight away.
He worked all night, and in the morning the wig was
ready.

  Jim carried it home. Then he tied it on his back and
climbed up the beanstalk.

The Giant loved his wig. "I look about a hundred years younger!" he said.

The Giant put on all his best clothes and danced around the room, beaming at himself in the mirror.

"It's terrific. I'm glad I didn't eat you." After a minute he said gruffly, "Now look, boy, you've done wonders. I feel happy again. You'd better go *now* before I feel like fried boy again."

Jim said good-bye fast and ran to the beanstalk. He slid
down it and landed in a heap. Above him the Giant
shouted, "Chop that beanstalk down or I might come down
and crunch you up with my new teeth." Seizing an ax,
Jim swung mightily and chopped down the beanstalk.

At the very moment the beanstalk fell, something else landed beside Jim with a thud. It was a giant gold coin wrapped in a giant piece of paper. On the paper was written:

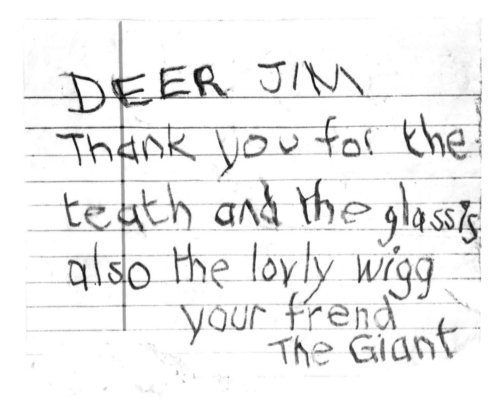

DEER JIM
Thank you for the
teath and the glass's
also the lovly wigg
            your frend
                The Giant

Jim ran inside and showed the giant gold coin to his mother.

"At last you can keep a coin for yourself," she said. Somewhere in the distance Jim heard a roar of giant laughter.